The Wagon Man

Written by Arthur Crowley

Illustrated by Annie Gusman

Houghton Mifflin Company Boston 1981

For Sue B. from Tim

For Tim from Annie

Library of Congress Cataloging in Publication Data
Crowley, Arthur.
    The Wagon Man.

    SUMMARY: The Wagon Man, who lures children away from
their homes to Tarry Town, is challenged by one of the
boys to a riddle game on which the fate of all the
children rests.
    [1. Riddles—Fiction.   2. Stories in rhyme]
I. Gusman, Annie. II. Title.
PZ8.3.C8863Wag [E]   80-23206
ISBN 0-395-30346-X

Text copyright © 1981 by Arthur Crowley
Illustrations copyright © 1981 by Annie Gusman

Printed in the United States of America

H 10 9 8 7 6 5 4 3 2 1

It came at dusk when all was still:
A hooded wagon rolling down
Quietly along the hill
That stood above the little town.

3

It waited there among the trees.
No one suspected what it was
Until a careless evening breeze
Spun devils in the summer dust.

That's when the little man appeared.
He wore a tattered coat of brown
And had a knobby wooden cane.
A man whom every parent feared
(the children could not speak his name):
The Wagon Man from Tarry Town.

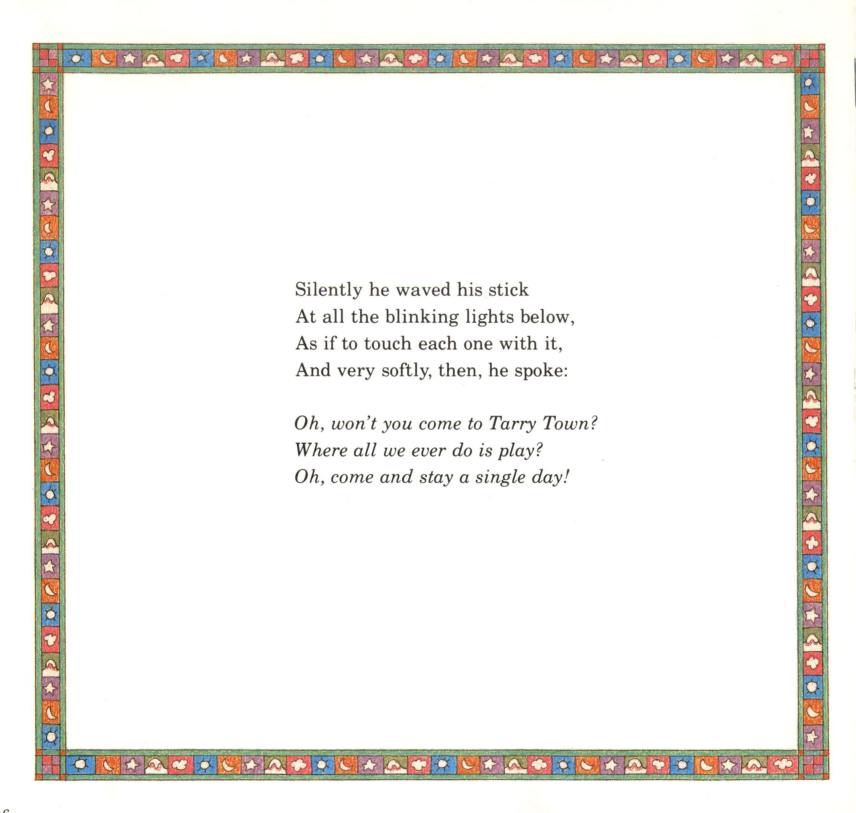

Silently he waved his stick
At all the blinking lights below,
As if to touch each one with it,
And very softly, then, he spoke:

Oh, won't you come to Tarry Town?
Where all we ever do is play?
Oh, come and stay a single day!

7

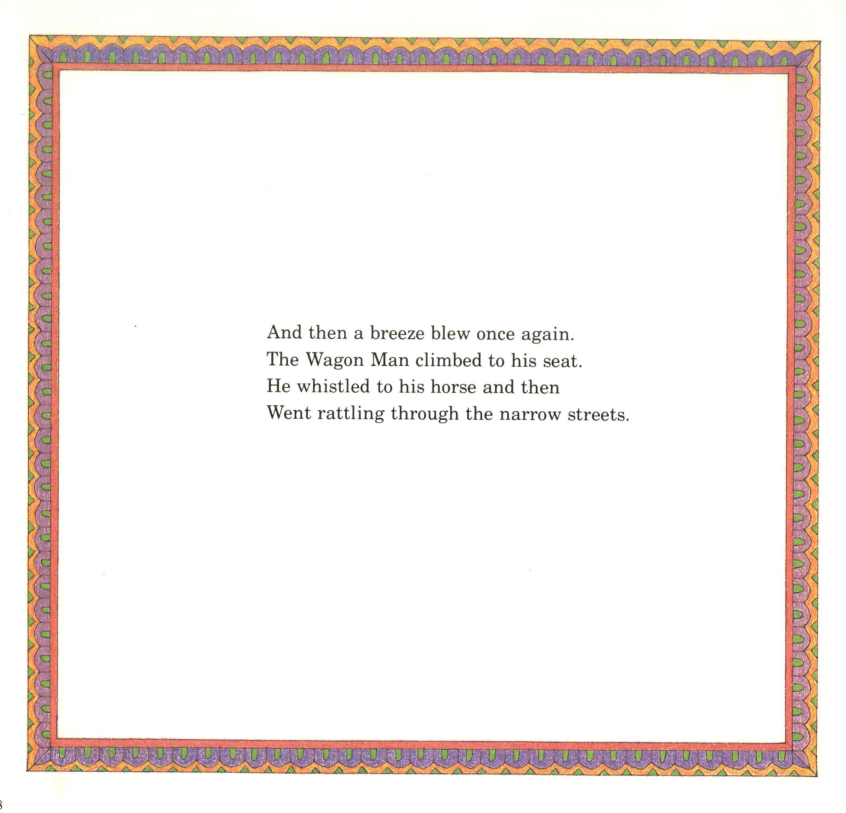

And then a breeze blew once again.
The Wagon Man climbed to his seat.
He whistled to his horse and then
Went rattling through the narrow streets.

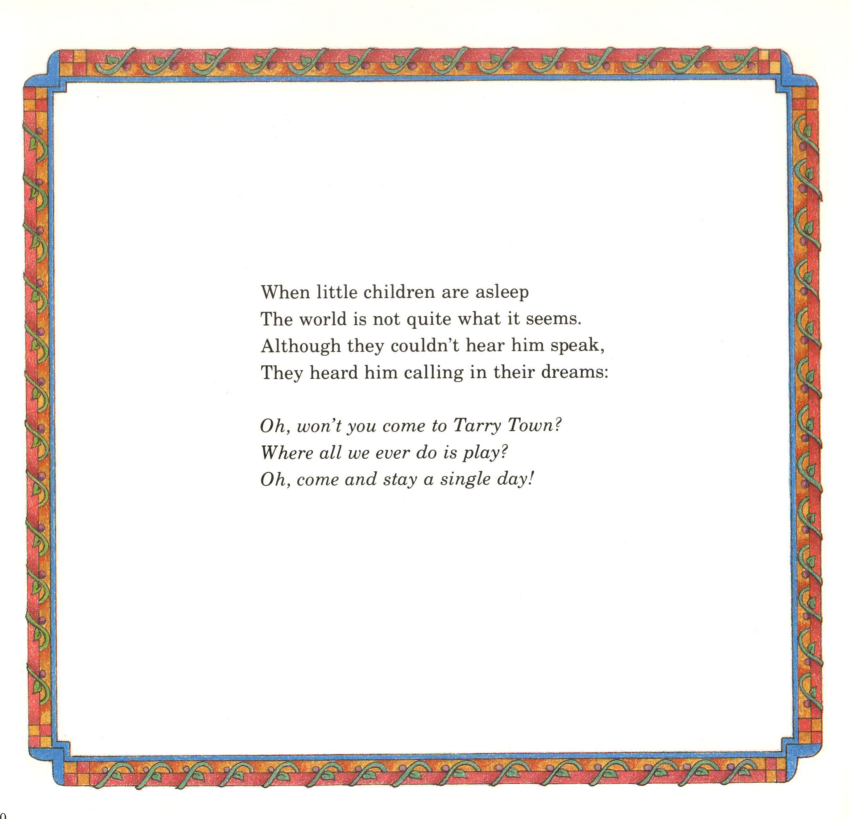

When little children are asleep
The world is not quite what it seems.
Although they couldn't hear him speak,
They heard him calling in their dreams:

Oh, won't you come to Tarry Town?
Where all we ever do is play?
Oh, come and stay a single day!

The children left their cozy beds.
From darkened homes they slipped away,
To heed the call inside their heads.
To Tarry Town! A single day!

They filled his wagon, one by one,
Those little shadows in the night.
In just a moment they were gone,
And rumbling slowly out of sight.

13

The stars went out, the moon went down,
The sun came up and made the day.
The little town awoke and found
The children all had run away!

Their parents didn't understand,
But then they saw the wagon's tracks.
"They've gone off with The Wagon Man!
"It means they're never coming back!"

14

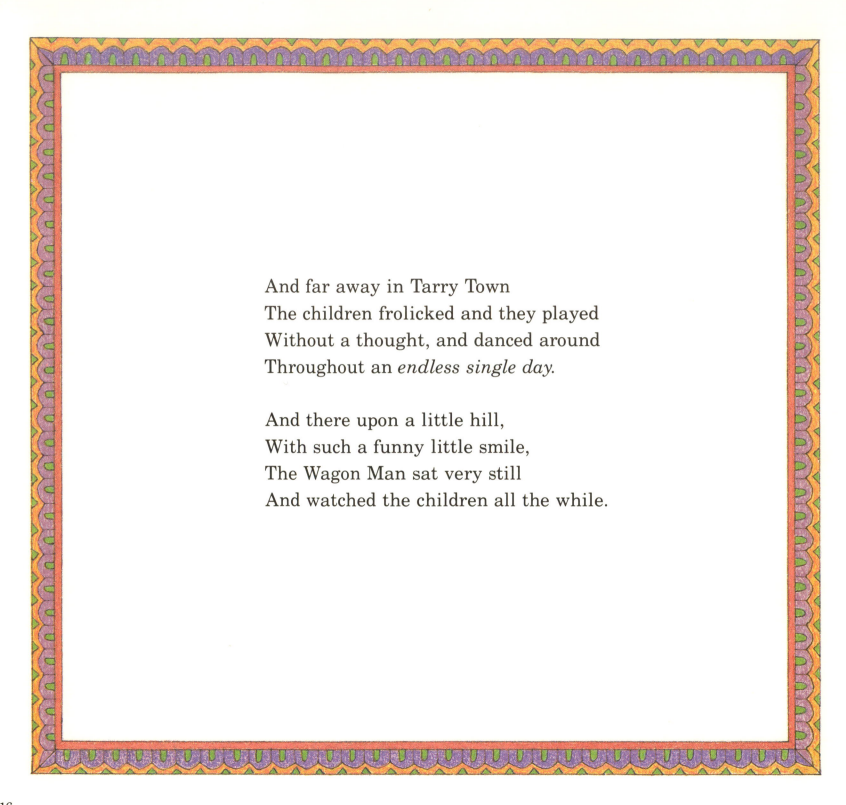

And far away in Tarry Town
The children frolicked and they played
Without a thought, and danced around
Throughout an *endless single day*.

And there upon a little hill,
With such a funny little smile,
The Wagon Man sat very still
And watched the children all the while.

From time to time his head would nod.
He seemed to hold them in his hand.
But then he noticed something odd.
It was a thing he hadn't planned.

There was one child, a little boy,
Who kept strange memories in his mind:
Of places, persons, favorite toys,
And feelings somehow left behind.

And all the time he laughed and ran
He saw his past as in a dream.
He saw but didn't understand.
He wondered what it all could mean.

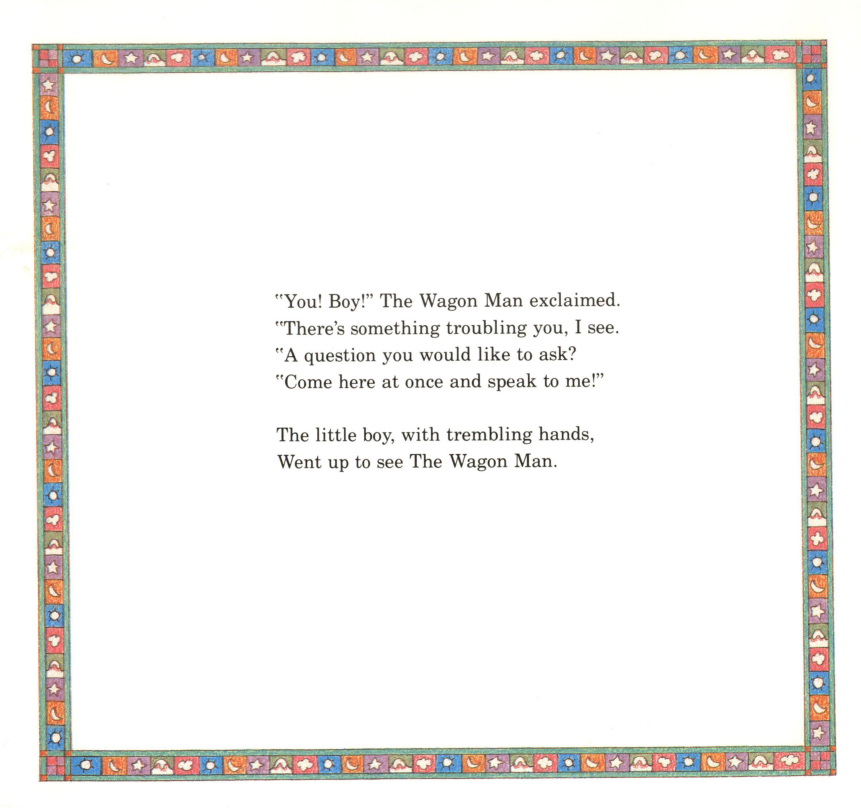

"You! Boy!" The Wagon Man exclaimed.
"There's something troubling you, I see.
"A question you would like to ask?
"Come here at once and speak to me!"

The little boy, with trembling hands,
Went up to see The Wagon Man.

The Wagon Man spoke in a hiss
And shriveled up his ugly face.
"You're wondering, you little fool,
"About a person or a place
"Or things that never did exist.
"The time has come for you and me
"To play a funny little game.
"When children do not wish to be
"In Tarry Town and stay all day,
"I give them each a single chance
"To play a game and get away.
"Listen well, the rules are these:
"Ask any question that you please,
"Explain my answer and you're free.
"But if you do not understand
"My riddle, you can never leave."

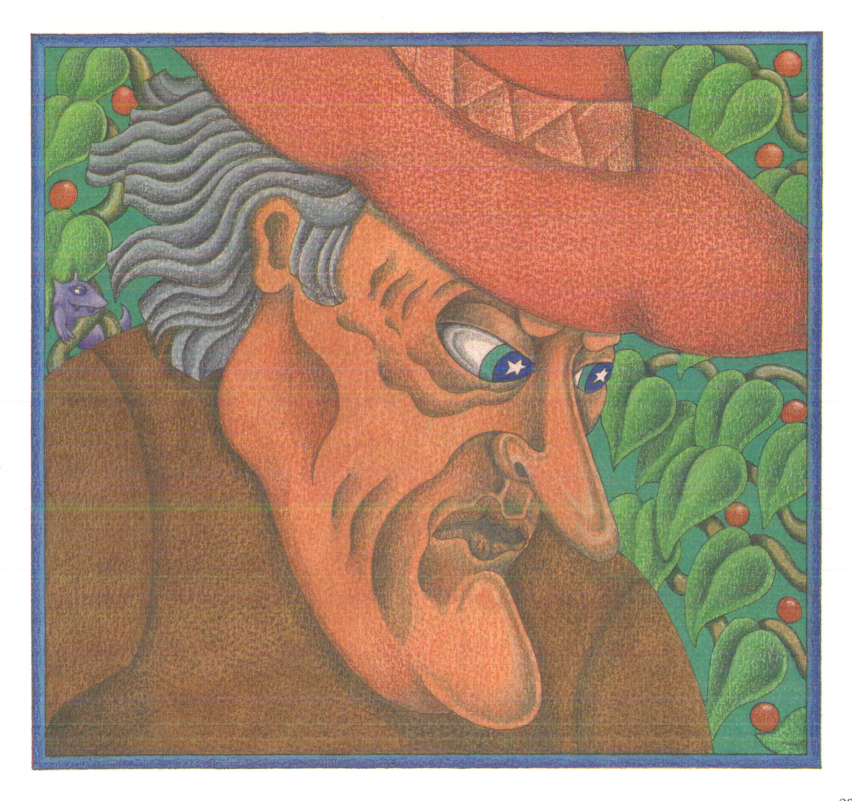

23

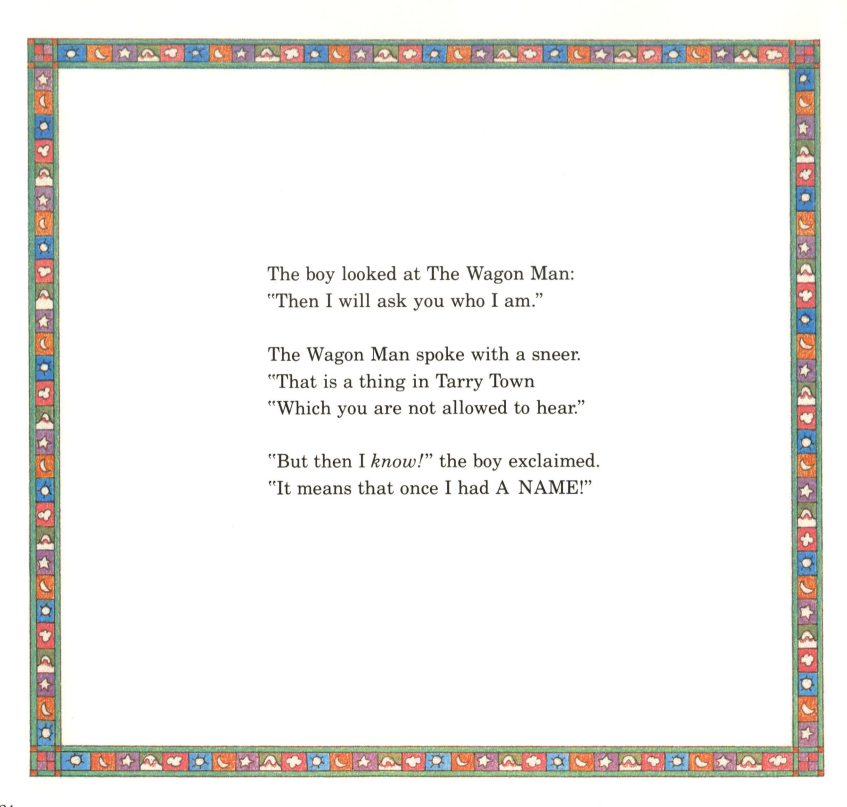

The boy looked at The Wagon Man:
"Then I will ask you who I am."

The Wagon Man spoke with a sneer.
"That is a thing in Tarry Town
"Which you are not allowed to hear."

"But then I *know!*" the boy exclaimed.
"It means that once I had A NAME!"

"Curses!" shrieked The Wagon Man.
"You've beaten me! Be off with you!"
But the boy said, "If I had a name,
"The other children had them, too.
"I'll play your guessing game again
"And I will make a deal with you.
"If I am wrong I have to stay,
"But if I'm right, they all come, too."

"Ask what question that you will,"
The Wagon Man said. "Certainly!
"And when you lose — and lose you will —
"You'll be here eternally!"

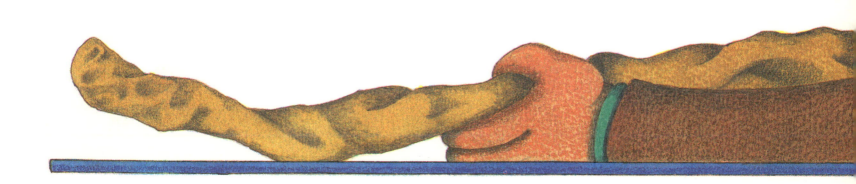

The boy said, "What I want to know is,
"If I leave, where shall I go?"

The Wagon Man said, "Do not start.
"You'll wander far. You'll be alone.
"Not finding it would break your heart."

The boy cried, "Then I have A HOME!
"And someone there who cares for me!
"Now set the other children free!"

The Wagon Man became enraged!
"You nasty boy!" he screamed. "You're *right!*
"Take the children! Go away!"
He then drove quickly out of sight.

So now the sun sinks slowly down.
The day is coming to an end.
The children are all safe and sound,
Back with their families again.

And yet, when summer days grow late,
Sometimes a rattling sound is heard,
A wagon seen among the trees.
No need to guess who it might be.

He never says a single word.
The Wagon Man just sits and waits.